CLEOPATRA'S SECRET

A TIME TRAVEL ADVENTURE

VICTORIA RUSH

VOLUME 4

RILEY'S TIME TRAVEL ADVENTURES -
BOOK 4

COPYRIGHT

ALSO BY VICTORIA RUSH

Adult Fairytales:

The Enchanted Forest: An Erotic Fairytale

The Land of Giants: An Erotic Fairytale

The Dragon's Lair: An Erotic Fairytale

Witch's Brew: An Erotic Fairytale

The Mage's Spell: An Erotic Fairytale

The Mermaid Lagoon: An Erotic Fairytale

The Coven: An Erotic Fairytale

Rapunzel: An Erotic Fairytale

The Seven Dwarfs: An Erotic Fairytale

The Land of Mutants: An Erotic Fairytale

The Erotic Temple: A Sexy Fairytale (Coming Soon)

Erotica Themed Bundles:

Voyeur: Lesbian Erotica Bundle

Public Affairs: A Lesbian Anthology

Futa Fantasies: The Ladyboy Collection

Threesomes: The Lesbian Collection

Threesomes - Volume 2: The Lesbian Collection

First Time: A Lesbian Anthology

Hedonism: An Erotic Anthology

Switch Hitters: Bisexual Erotica

Taboo Erotica: The Lesbian Series

BDSM: The Lesbian Collection

Party Games: The Erotic Collection

Party Games 2: The Erotic Collection

All Girl 1: Lesbian Erotica Bundle

All Girl 2: Lesbian Erotica Bundle

All Girl 3: Lesbian Erotica Bundle

All Girl 4: Lesbian Erotica Bundle

Erotic Fairytale Bundles:

Clover's Fantasy Adventures: Books 1 - 5

Clover's Fantasy Adventures: Books 6 - 10

Erotic Fantasy:

Pirate's Bounty: A Time Travel Adventure

Wild West: A Time Travel Adventure

Private Riley: A Time Travel Adventure

Cleopatra's Secret: A Time Travel Adventure

Bounty Hunter 2125: A Time Travel Adventure

Ninja Assassin: A Time Travel Adventure

The 300: A Time Travel Adventure

Arabian Nights: An Erotic Fairytale (coming soon...)

Steamy Time Travel Bundles:

Riley's Time Travel Adventures: Books 1 - 5

Lesbian Erotica:

The Dinner Party: Lesbian Voyeur Erotica

The Darkroom: Bisexual Voyeur Erotica

Naked Yoga: Lesbian Transgender Erotica

Nude Cruise: Bisexual Voyeur Erotica

Rush Hour: Taboo Public Sex

The Girl Next Door: First Time Lesbian Erotic Romance

Girls' Camp: Lesbian Group Sex

Wet Dream: Ladyboy Fantasy Erotica

The Convent: Taboo Sex with a Nun

Sex Robot: A Dream Sex Machine

The Personal Trainer: Getting Pumped at the Gym

The Dominatrix: BDSM Lesbian Domination

Webcam Chat: Lesbian Online Sex

Paint Me: A Kinky Bodypainting Workshop

The Toy Party: Girls Sharing Sex Toys

The Costume Party: Strapping One On

Swedish Sauna: Lesbian Group Sex

The Therapist: Taboo Lesbian Erotica

Elevator Shaft: Bisexual Threesomes Erotica

Ladyboy: Lesbian Transgender Erotica

Peep Show: Lesbian Voyeur Erotica

The Dare: Public Sex Erotica

Maid Service: Lesbian Threesomes Erotica

The Hitchhiker: First Time Lesbian Erotica

The Housesitter: Spycam Lesbian Erotica

The Spa: Lesbian Group Orgy

Parlor Games: Blindfold Sex Party

The Exchange Student: First Time Lesbian Erotica

The Hostel: Bisexual Group Erotica

The Harem: Lesbian Erotic Romance

The Orient Express: Lesbian Voyeur Erotica

The First Lady: A Forbidden Lesbian Erotic Romance

The Slave: Lesbian BDSM Erotica

The Masseuse: Lesbian Sensuous Erotica

Too Close for Comfort: Lesbian Forbidden Erotica

Naked Twister: A Wild Party Game

Lexi: The Sex App (Lesbian Fantasy Erotica)

Call Girl: Lesbian Bisexual Threesomes Erotica

Circle Jill: Lesbian Masturbation Workshop

The Viewing Room: Masturbation Voyeur Erotica

Spin the Bottle: A Kinky Party Game

The Hair Salon: Lesbian Voyeur Erotica

Tribadism 1: Girls Only Sex Workshop

Tribadism 2: The Art of Scissoring

Tribadism 3: Threeway Hookups

The Kiss: A Game of Oral Sex

Pledge Week: Sorority Sisters

Carny Games 1: A Wild Sex Party

Carny Games 2: A Kinky Sex Party

Carny Games 3: An Erotic Sex Party

Dreamscape: An Artificial Reality Game

Glory Hole: Guess Who's On the Other Side

Joy Ride: A Late Night Erotic Bus Trip

The Blind Girl: An Erotic Romance(Coming Soon)

Lesbian Erotica Bundles:

Jade's Erotic Adventures: Books 1 - 5

Jade's Erotic Adventures: Books 6 - 10

Jade's Erotic Adventures: Books 11 - 15

Jade's Erotic Adventures: Books 16 - 20

Jade's Erotic Adventures: Books 21 - 25

Jade's Erotic Adventures: Books 26 - 30

Jade's Erotic Adventures: Books 31 - 35

Jade's Erotic Adventures: Books 36 - 40

Jade's Erotic Adventures: Books 41 - 45

Jade's Erotic Adventures: Books 46 - 50

Fifty Shades of Jade: Superbundle

Standalone Stories:

The Polynesian Girl: A Lesbian EroticRomance

For the uninhibited...

WANT TO AMP UP YOUR SEX LIFE?

Sign up for my newsletter to receive more free books and other steamy stuff. Discover a hundred different ways to wet your whistle!

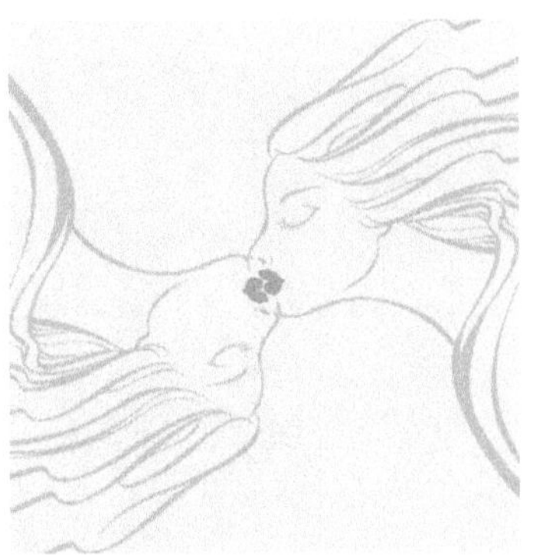

Victoria Rush Erotica

1

———

While Riley tumbled through the time machine portal wondering where she'd land next, her thoughts flashed back to her WWII adventure. She prayed that her German handler would recover and explain to her commanding officer that she was still alive. But soon her thoughts turned to her next destination. She had no way of knowing where her time machine would drop her, but if it was anything like her last three escapades, she'd have little more than her wits and knowledge of world history to keep her out of trouble.

When she landed on a marble floor in a large palace, she picked herself up and walked over to the nearest window, noticing three giant pyramids standing in the distance.

Egypt, she said to herself, recognizing the site of ancient Giza. *But what year?*

Suddenly, a servant girl wearing a thin tunic approached her, peering at her with pinched eyebrows.

"Who are you?" she said in a strange language Riley had never heard before.

"My name's Riley," Riley said, speaking the dialect seamlessly.

"I'll have to announce you to the queen," the servant girl said. "Cleopatra doesn't like unwanted visitors in the palace."

Cleopatra? Riley thought, shaking her head. *Now there's someone I thought I'd never meet.*

As the girl led Riley through the labyrinthine palace, she peered up at the tall columns and gilded ceilings painted with Hellenistic frescoes, bulging her eyes.

So this is what Cleopatra's palace looked like before it sank to the bottom of the Mediterranean, she thought.

Various guards dressed in Roman military uniforms peered at her curiously, and Riley reflected back on her cursory knowledge of Roman history. The Romans had an on-and-off-again interest in the area of North Africa and the Middle East known as the Fertile Crescent, but it wasn't until the time of Caesar that Egypt officially became a client state.

Ok, she thought. *So this places me somewhere in the first century B.C. If Cleopatra is still the queen, then this narrows it down to the years 50 to 30 B.C.*

The servant girl led Riley into a large chamber with a sunken bath and a terrace overlooking the Mediterranean Sea. A dark-haired woman wearing an embroidered silk robe and long, golden earrings lay on a padded lounge chair, surrounded by a group of attendants attending to her hands, feet, and hair. The woman looked up when she saw Riley and the servant girl entering the room, squinting at Riley's unusual attire.

"What is it, Iras?" she said, speaking Greek. "Can't you see that I'm busy?"

"I'm sorry, my queen," the servant girl said, bowing softly. "I found this interloper in the palace and thought I should ask how you would like her disposed before handing her over to the guards."

Cleopatra glanced at Riley's twentieth-century clothes, then she shook her head.

"An interloper?" she said, looking at Riley. "How did you get past my guards?"

Riley peered at Cleopatra blankly, unsure how to explain her improbable circumstances. There was no way the queen would believe she came through time from the distant future, likely to lock her up in an asylum, thinking she'd lost her mind.

"I–was just admiring the palace and guess I got lost," she said in perfect Greek, amazed at how her time machine enabled her to speak any language.

"Lost?" Cleopatra said, turning toward the servant girl. "Where did you find her?"

"In the East Wing, in one of the guest quarters," Iras said.

"I don't remember *inviting* you as one of my guests," Cleopatra said, narrowing her eyes.

Riley paused for a moment to appraise the beautiful queen lounging on her chair. She had a long slender nose, bright brown eyes highlighted with iridescent eye shadow, and full sensuous lips that sparkled whenever she spoke. But even more beautiful than her face was her long, shapely figure. With perfectly sculpted legs, graceful arms, and a deep cleavage peeking through the slit in her robe, Riley was mesmerized by the celebrated queen.

"I'm sorry madam–I mean, *queen*," she stammered, thinking her best hope was to get out of there as quickly as possible. "I'll be taking my leave with your permission."

"Not so fast," Cleopatra said, motioning for the guards to block the exits. "We don't just let strangers waltz in and out of here, unannounced. You don't look like you're from around here."

"I'm from the west," Riley said, knowing that America wouldn't even be discovered for over a thousand years.

"You're light-skinned," the queen nodded. "Are you from Gaul?"

"Britannia," Riley said, trying to remember what Britain was called during ancient times.

"Britannia?" Cleopatra said. "You're a long way from home, for someone so young. How did you manage to come this far?"

"It's a bit of a long story," Riley sighed, knowing she was fighting a losing battle to explain herself.

"I imagine it is," Cleopatra smiled, noticing the drops of sweat forming on Riley's brow. "So now the question is, what to do with you? We can't just put you on a boat and sail you thousands of miles back to your homeland."

Riley hesitated, remembering how she'd helped her previous hosts using her knowledge of world history and modern military strategy.

"I'm quite resourceful," Riley said, hoping to avoid an ignominious fate. "I'm sure I could be useful to you in a number of ways."

"Oh?" the queen said, darting her eyes over Riley's lithe, athletic figure. "What skills would a little girl like you have that I might find useful?"

Riley glanced at the queen's attendants, struggling to come up with a plausible role.

"I'm pretty good with hair," she said, remembering how much she and her sister liked to experiment with braiding and curling each other's locks when they were younger. "And I have some knowledge of world history that might come in handy."

"World history?" the queen said, squinting at Riley suspiciously. "How far back can you go for someone as young as you?"

"I might surprise you," Riley said.

"I'll tell you what," Cleopatra smiled. "If you can tell me the name of my great-great-grandfather, I might let you live."

Riley gulped as she closed her eyes, trying to reflect back on her knowledge of Greek and Egyptian history. When she looked back up, she recognized a bust of Alexander the Great sitting on a pedestal leading out to the terrace, remembering that Cleopatra was part of the Ptolemaic Dynasty.

"If I remember correctly," she said. "You're descended from the Macedonian Greek general Ptolemy the First, who was a military confidant of Alexander the Great, after whom the city of Alexandria is named."

Cleopatra tilted her head to the side, darting her eyes between her attendants, surprised that this stranger from a faraway land could know so much about her.

"That's impressive, indeed," she nodded, motioning for the guards to stand down. "I have no idea who you are or how you got here, but there's something about you that I find intriguing. I will allow you to stay on as a servant for the time being. I'm sure we can find *something* useful for you to do around here."

Then she motioned to the girl who had found Riley.

"Iras will show you to the servants' quarters, where you can change into something more appropriate. I will call for you in due course."

"Thank you, my queen," Riley said, sighing in relief.

"Wait," Cleopatra said, as Riley turned to leave. "What's your name?"

"Riley."

"Well, Riley," Cleopatra smiled, peering down at Riley's full breasts propped up by her tight-fitting bra under her thin blouse. "Something tells me we'll be uncovering a few *more* surprises about you before too long."

While she followed Iras to the lower level of the palace, Riley suddenly became aware of the dampness in her panties. Unbeknownst to her while she was fighting to save her skin, she'd found the glamorous Egyptian queen quite alluring.

Eat your heart out, Elizabeth Taylor, she grinned to herself. *You can't hold a candle to the real thing.*

2

———

When Iras led Riley into the servant quarters on the lower level, she pulled open an armoire, handing her a silk robe.

"Here," she said. "This is what the queen likes her female attendants to wear."

Riley peered at the skimpy gown, wrinkling her forehead.

"What am I supposed to wear *underneath* it?"

"Nothing," Iras smiled. "Cleopatra prefers her attendants to be accessible at all times."

Accessible? Riley thought, feeling her pussy throbbing at the idea of getting naked with the queen.

She rubbed her fingers over the satin fabric, admiring the soft sheen on the claret-colored gown.

It's rare to find women's robes made from real silk these days. This would go for upwards of a grand in the high-end boutiques in Boston.

She removed her western clothes and placed them on one of the two cots in the small room, then she slipped the robe over her naked body. After cinching the belt around her narrow waist, she stepped in front of the wardrobe mirror, nodding approvingly.

"What do you think?" she said to Iras, standing nearby.

"Much better," Iras said, glancing at Riley's firm breasts shaping the front of the gown like two mountain peaks. "I'm sure the queen will approve."

"Is this where I'll be sleeping?" Riley said, glancing toward the two beds.

"Yes. You'll be bunking with me, unless Cleopatra decides to relocate you.

"Where are the restrooms?"

"Down the hall and to the left," Iras said, pointing through the door. "There's a pantry on the opposite side of the hall where you can help yourself to some food if you like."

Riley peered at the pretty servant girl, thankful she'd discovered her trespassing in the palace instead of one of the guards.

"Thanks for looking after me," she said.

"I'll see you a little later in the day," Iras smiled. "I have to return to my duties now."

"What exactly are your duties, if I may ask?"

"I'm kind of an all-purpose servant, looking after whatever needs the queen may have. Usually, it involves running errands and acting as a messenger between her other attendants."

"Well thanks for running *interference* for me," Riley said. "I'll look forward to seeing you when your duties are finished."

As Iras turned to exit the room, Riley glanced at her shapely ass, highlighted by her thin and tight-fitting tunic. Up to this point, she'd been so distracted by the opulent surroundings of the palace, she'd barely given the servant girl a second glance. Knowing they'd be sharing the small sleeping quarters made her pussy twitch. But first, she had a more urgent matter to attend to.

Following Iras's directions, she exited the room and headed in the direction of the women's washroom. When she entered the large communal chamber, her eyes widened in surprised. Lined from floor to ceiling in white alabaster marble, the room sparkled with sunlight streaming in through the overhead skylights. A stream of water trickled from carved stone pipes near the top of an oversize shower stall and from an angled trough under the marble vanity. Riley peered at a line of stalls covered with ornamental wooden doors and opened one, smiling in relief. Under a limestone bench with a one-foot diameter hole, she glanced down, noticing another stream of water flowing under the commode.

"Thank God," she sighed, sitting down on the limestone seat to empty her bladder. "Why is it the Egyptians could figure out how to rig a toilet with running water, but the Americans of the Wild West couldn't do it almost two thousand years later?"

Then she peered at the sides of the stall, noticing no dispensers for toilet paper.

"Okay," she nodded. "I suppose it'll be a while before they invent *toilet paper*. I guess we're expected to wash up in the showers instead. It's cleaner that way, anyhow."

When she finished her business, she hung her robe on a hook on the wall, then she stepped under one of the flowing pipes jutting out from the shower wall. The water was surprisingly warm, and noticing what looked like a bar of soap resting in an alcove, she picked it up and held it to her nose.

"Lavender and rosemary," she smiled, shaking her head.

"I could get used to living in this place. It's a nice step up from the pirate ship and the Wild West brothel."

While she lathered her body with the perfumy soap, her hand slipped between her thighs, imagining herself with the beautiful queen. As her pleasure began to mount, she thought she heard footsteps in the outer hall, and she decided to stop, knowing she'd be fully exposed if someone walked into the lavatory.

After she finished cleaning up, she headed to the other side of the hall, where she found an open lunchroom with fresh fruit and cheese laid out on a long table flanked with stone benches. She leaned over and sampled the buffet, widening her eyes in delight.

"Oh my God," she grunted, gulping down the food. "These are the juiciest figs and pomegranates I've ever tasted. And this cheese–is that *parmesan*? If this is how the servants live in this place, I can only imagine how spoiled the *queen* must be–"

Suddenly, Iras entered the pantry from the other side and Riley glanced up, wiping the dripping pomegranate juice from her chin.

"Sorry," she said, wiping her hands with a linen napkin resting on the table. "It's been a while since I've eaten anything, and these pomegranates are to die for."

"I'm glad you're enjoying them," Iras smiled. "But don't get too gorged on food. The queen would like to see you in her personal bath."

"*Bath?*" Riley said, turning her head. "What does she want me *there* for?"

"I'm not sure," Iras said. "But you'd better clean yourself up before heading up there. I'm not sure she'll appreciate your sticky fingers as much as you seem to be right now."

3

After Riley washed up, she followed Iras up three levels until she reemerged in Cleopatra's boudoir. This time, the queen was lounging alone in her sunken bathtub, surrounded by floating rose petals. When she saw Iras enter the room, she turned her head and smiled.

"Thank you, Iras," she said. "You can leave us alone now. Please close the door on the way out."

"Yes, my queen," Iras said, bowing as she backed out the door.

"You cleaned up nicely," Cleopatra nodded, glancing at Riley's silk robe. "That color becomes you."

"Thank you," Riley said. "It's been a while since I've had a shower, and this material feels wonderful against my freshly washed skin."

The queen peered at Riley's curvy figure in her tight-fitting robe, noticing her nipples darting the front of the soft fabric.

"You said you had some experience styling hair," she

said. "Do you think you can attend to me while I'm lying in the tub?"

Riley noticed a soft towel propped under her head at the end of the tub and nodded.

"I think so. If you don't mind my sitting behind you."

"Not at all," Cleopatra smiled, beckoning Riley with a curled finger. "Come, let's continue our conversation."

Riley walked over toward the tub then sat down in a cross-legged position behind the queen's resting head.

"Um..." she said, hesitant to disturb her impeccably styled locks. "Do you have a preference for how you'd like your hair prepared?"

"I'm a bit bored with this bowl cut my stylists seem so enamored with. Why don't you use your imagination and try something different?"

Riley paused for a moment, trying to imagine what style might best befit the glamorous queen. Then she lifted her arms, gently separating the back of her hair into two equal sections. She clasped the segment on the left side and began twisting and joining it into a long braid, slowly working toward the end. As she methodically threaded her fingers between Cleopatra's locks, she glanced at the water, trying to catch a glimpse of the queen's naked body. But she was submerged just far enough under the surface to keep the tips of her breasts tantalizingly out of view under the blanket of rose petals.

"You still haven't told me how you managed to travel all this way from Britannia," Cleopatra said, peering over her shoulder at Riley.

Riley stopped her braiding while she contemplated how to explain her improbable story of traveling through time using modern twenty-first-century technology.

"I—had a little help from a friend," she stammered.

"A sailor?" the queen said.

"In a manner of speaking."

"So you know how to *sail* also?"

"I've had some practice," Riley nodded, reflecting back on her 17th-century pirate adventure.

"Your talents seem to belie your youthful age," the queen said, lapping some bath water over the top of her breasts with her hands.

Riley glanced down, noticing the rose petals parting and Cleopatra's pointed teats jutting out of the water temporarily.

"I suppose," she shuddered. "I've had a little more life experience than most people my age."

"It would have taken considerable resources for you to manage such a long journey," Cleopatra said. "Are you descended from the noble class?"

"I don't think so," Riley chuckled. "I just seem to have a knack for being in the right place at the wrong time."

"You're so *mysterious*," Cleopatra said. "I like mysterious. So much more to discover while we peel back the layers."

"I'm a pretty simple girl, really," Riley said, reaching the end of the first braid and pinching it together with her fingers. "Do you have an elastic band or a clasp to hold your hair?"

"A what?" the queen said, tilting up her head.

"Sorry," Riley said, remembering that everyday implements that modern people had taken for granted still wouldn't be invented for hundreds of years. "I meant some kind of pin. Something small and narrow that can be threaded through your hair."

"Yes," Cleopatra said, pointing toward a narrow hallway leading to the interior of her chamber. "I have some in my private washing quarters. If you head down that corridor and turn left at the end, you'll find my lavatory. There should be some in the drawer under the left wash basin."

"Okay," Riley said, following her line of sight. "Would you mind holding the ends of this strand to keep your hair from unraveling?"

Cleopatra lifted her left arm and Riley guided her hand toward the end of the braid, pinching her fingers softly over the tufted end. The sensation of touching the queen's skin was electrifying, and Riley could feel her pussy twitching, so close to her dripping hand.

"Here?" Cleopatra asked, caressing Riley's hand with one of her fingers.

"Yes," Riley said, lifting herself up with wobbly knees. "I'll be right back."

"Don't take too long," the queen said, peering at Riley's tight ass as she headed toward her interior quarters. "I might turn into a prune if I stay in this water much longer."

"I don't think there's much danger of that," Riley said, turning her head to smile at the queen before she disappeared down the hall.

4

When Riley entered Cleopatra's private washroom, she gasped, bulging her eyes in shock. Easily five times the size of the servants' restroom, it was bedecked in gleaming marble and solid gold fixtures, with sunlight beaming in from the overhead portals and fresh water streaming from all the fixtures. But this one also had a huge makeup table, a large glass-enclosed shower, two commodes, a separate bidet, and a wide double vanity framed with a wall-length volcanic glass mirror.

Okay, she nodded. *So this is how the other half lives. Nice gig if you can swing it.*

She peered toward the double sinks decorated with gold faucets and pulled out the drawer under the left basin. Inside, she noticed a gold-embossed hair brush and comb, various oils and powders, and a small gold jar. When she opened the jar, she noticed a collection of silver pins and she plucked up a dozen, dropping them into the inner pocket of her robe.

Before she left the room, she paused, peering toward the

other wash basin. She hadn't seen any sign of the queen's companion, but she knew from her study of Egyptian history that Cleopatra had affairs with both Julius Caesar and Marc Antony. Turning her head to make sure no one else was nearby, she pulled open the other drawer, noticing a collection of male grooming instruments, including a straight-edge razor.

So, which one is it? she wondered, closing the drawer. She still wasn't sure of the precise year, so she had no way of knowing who was her a present lover.

When she returned to the main chamber, Cleopatra narrowed her eyes when she saw Riley's flushed face.

"Did you have any trouble finding what you needed?" she said.

"No," Riley said. "They were exactly where you said."

"It's a good thing my husband is away on state business," the queen smiled. "Otherwise, he might have been surprised to see a pretty girl fishing around our private belongings."

Riley was tempted to ask the queen more details about her husband, but she knew that would be overstepping her bounds.

"Will he be away long?" she said.

"He's expected back later today," the queen nodded. "Returning after another triumphant military campaign in the Balkans. I'm sure he'll be interested to meet the latest member of our household."

"I'll look forward to that," Riley said, pinning the long braid to the side of the queen's head in a semi-crown arrangement.

As she repeated the procedure on the other side of the queen's hair, Cleopatra continued to make small talk with her, becoming more and more suggestive with each passing minute.

"I couldn't help notice when you went into the wash-room that your legs are more toned than the other servants," she said, glancing up at Riley with her huge brown eyes. "How did you manage to come by such a comely figure?"

Riley gazed back at her with flushed cheeks, feeling the loose strands of Cleopatra's hair caressing the front of her pussy through the parted robe between her crossed knees.

"I like to exercise to keep fit," she said, biting her lip to stifle a groan. "I believe a strong body blends with a strong mind, and vice versa."

"That's a wise code to live by," Cleopatra nodded. "But how do you participate in this exercise? I've found this is a habit normally reserved for men."

Riley hesitated again, knowing how ridiculous it would be to talk about indoor gyms and yoga studios even before the time of the original Olympic Games.

"It's mostly from running and calisthenics," she said. "I like the way it makes me feel."

"Yes," the queen purred. "It always feels good to get the blood circulating to the extremities."

Riley stopped her braiding activity for a moment, feeling a dribble of lubricating running down the inside of her thigh.

Is the Queen of Egypt flirting with me? she thought to herself.

Thinking it best not to return the queen's advances so directly, she continued squeezing and caressing her hair until she completed the second braid, curling it around the other side of her head to form a tufted crown.

"All done," she announced, dragging the tips of her fingers through the rest of her hair and tidy up the loose ends.

"How does it look?" Cleopatra said, sitting up and turning around to face Riley.

Riley couldn't help stealing a glance at her exposed breasts sitting high on her chest, colored with huge brown nipples the size of ancient medallions.

"Beautiful," Riley nodded, peering back up at her hair. "Very befitting a queen, if I do say so myself."

"Do me a favor, will you?" Cleopatra said. "Can you fetch my makeup mirror from my dressing table in the washroom? I don't want to get out of the tub quite yet, but I'm dying to see your handiwork."

"Of course," Riley said, pulling her robe closed as she stood up. But before she had a chance to do so, she noticed the queen staring at her exposed bush with its glistening tips.

"Oh, and one other thing," Cleopatra said as Riley turned in the direction of her private quarters. "There's a razor in the drawer under the second sink. I think I'd like to clean up the *lower* half of my body to make it as pretty as the top."

Holy shit, Riley muttered as she scurried back in the direction of the queen's rest room. *I seriously need to get off as soon as I'm back in my private quarters. That is, assuming the queen doesn't slice my throat when she sees what I've done with her hair.*

When she returned to the tub, she kneeled down in front of the queen, handing her the makeup mirror. Cleopatra held it up to her face then her eyes widened, beaming in surprise.

"It's beautiful, Riley," she nodded. "It's like I'm wearing a crown made out of my own hair. I can't wait to show Marc Antony when he returns from his military campaign."

"I'm glad you like it, my queen," Riley smiled, breathing a sigh of relief, excited to meet her husband.

5

───────

"**I**n fact, I like it so much," Cleopatra said, gazing at Riley with a twinkle in her eye. "I'd hate for you to stop there. I don't suppose you know how to work similar wonders down *below*?"

"Down below?" Riley said, glancing at the queen's submerged body.

"You know, my *private* area," Cleopatra smiled, lifting her body slowly out of the water. "It seems a shame to have the hair on my head so perfectly sculpted while the hair over my pussy is so wild and messy."

"Um–" Riley stammered, temporarily tongue-tied while staring at the queen's dripping body as she held the straight edge in her shaking hand. "How would you like me to do that, exactly?"

"Very carefully, of course," Cleopatra said, resting her ass on the edge of the tub and slowly spreading her legs apart. "But I think this time, *you* should be the one resting in the tub. This time it's *my* turn to steal glances at you while you groom me."

As she began to pull off her robe, Riley could feel her heart pounding a million miles an hour.

"As you wish, my queen," she said, sinking her naked body into the warm, scented water.

Before she submerged under the surface, Cleopatra darted her eyes over her figure. Then Riley kneeled gently in front of her while the queen raised her feet, placing them on opposite the sides of the tub.

Riley's eyes bulged, looking at the queen's pink folds, spread apart like the petals of a flower, framed with dark tendrils of baby's breath.

"I'm not quite sure where to begin," she gulped, reluctant to touch the queen with the razor-sharp instrument.

"Perhaps near the top," Cleopatra smiled. "Then you can work your way down to the more sensitive areas. We wouldn't want you cutting off more than you need to, would we?"

Riley peered down, noticing a drop of lubrication dripping out of the queen's pussy and down the crack of her ass.

"Exactly how much would you like trimmed?" she said.

"I'm not sure," the queen teased. "How much is common among girls where you come from?"

"A lot of women shave themselves completely bare," Riley said. "But I'm not sure that would be appropriate, given your position–"

"Why not?" Cleopatra said. "You know how men are always fantasizing about young girls. I'm sure my husband would find it very arousing to see me this way when we retire to our bed chamber."

"Are you sure?" Riley said. "Because it will take many weeks to grow back."

"The longer it takes for you to trim me, the longer I get to view your pretty figure," Cleopatra smiled, staring at Riley's dripping tits sticking out of the water while she kneeled between her legs. "Men aren't the *only* ones who like young girls."

"Okay," Riley said, happy that her hips at least were submerged under the surface of the water so the queen couldn't see how wet she'd become listening to her increasingly lascivious comments.

While she leaned toward the queen's dripping sex, she gulped, shaking the straight edge in her hand. Normally, she would use a modern safety razor to trim her pubic hair, reserving an electric shaver for the more sensitive areas around her labia. But this time, she'd have nothing but a steady hand and her good eyesight to stop her from nicking the queen's most sensitive parts.

As she tilted the edge forty-five degrees downwards, she slowly swiped the razor down over the queen's wet pubic hair, creating small channels shaped like the freshly shoveled snow on her Boston driveway.

Thank God, she sighed to herself, thankful that the long soak in the tub had softened the queen's thick pubic hair.

"Mmm," Cleopatra purred as Riley gently dragged the razor over the top of her mound. "That feels exquisite. We'll have to do this more often. This feels so much more sensuous than the scissors my normal groomers use."

"So far, so good," Riley exhaled, peering up at the queen. "But we still haven't gotten to the hard part."

"I can hardly wait," Cleopatra grinned, watching Riley while she scraped the pubic hair off her mound. "I'm getting incredibly turned on watching you do this."

"That makes two of us," Riley said, undulating her body softly in the rolling water.

"Your breasts are very beautiful," Cleopatra said, staring at Riley's tits as she leaned over her crotch. "They're very full and firm. I remember when my bosom used to look like that."

Riley peered up for a moment, glancing at the queen's pointed tubers, quivering gently as her stomach flexed in and out in obvious excitement.

"Your breasts are magnificent, if you don't mind my saying," Riley smiled. "They're very unique and sensuous. I'd die to have a figure like yours."

"Well, that would take all the fun out of it, wouldn't it?" Cleopatra chuckled. "We can't have you dying while you're still so young. Or at least until I've had a chance to sample some *more* of your hidden talents."

Riley stopped her blade near the base of the queen's mound, staring at her swollen clit, pressing out from its hood like a little pig in a blanket.

"I just hope I can survive long enough to trim the rest of your pubic hair before slicing off something I'm not supposed to," she said.

"Just go slow and easy, like you did with the rest of me," Cleopatra said. "And I'm sure there'll be no need to take such drastic measures."

While she held her breath, Riley turned the razor sideways, beginning to scrape off the short hairs on the side of the queen's outer labia.

"You know," Cleopatra smiled, noticing the sheen of perspiration forming on Riley's forehead. "Some tribes in the southern provinces cut off a girl's external sex organ before they reach maturity. They think it will keep them more chaste for their husbands."

"It's barbaric," Riley said, tightening her jaw at the practice known as female circumcision. "Taking away a woman's pleasure even before she's had a chance to experience sexual intimacy. I can only imagine how painful the procedure must be."

"I couldn't agree more," Cleopatra said. "But I have little control over what people do in the privacy of their own homes, so far out in the wilderness."

"I suppose so," Riley said, scraping away the last loose threads around the queen's twitching clit. "The only thing that will stop it is proper education and improved prosperity. It will take a long time before women gain the same rights as men."

She pulled back from the queen's shaved pussy, breathing a sigh of relief.

"It's all done," she said, smiling at the bald crotch.

Cleopatra peered down then ran her right hand softly over her smooth skin.

"My God," she grunted. "That feels heavenly. Even better than when I normally touch myself."

She curled her fingers and began circling her clit, moaning as she tilted her head back.

"I'm so happy you fell into my lap," Cleopatra said, peering into Riley's eyes while she caressed herself. "Literally and figuratively. What other talents have you been holding out on me?"

Riley glanced down, watching the queen rubbing her dripping cunt more excitedly, then she licked her lips suggestively.

"Well, there's one that I particularly enjoy, but I'd never presume to touch the queen so intimately..."

Cleopatra lifted her fingers from her dripping pussy, then she extended them toward Riley's face, slipping them into her mouth. Riley closed her eyes while she sucked on them gently, rolling her hips sensuously in the tub.

"Please," Cleopatra panted, spreading her knees wider apart. "I've been dying to feel your lips on my sex from the moment I laid eyes on you."

6

Riley peered down at the queen's glistening snatch, then she edged her face closer until her lips enveloped her tumescent bulb. Cleopatra grabbed Riley's hair and threw her head back, pulling her harder against her pussy. As Riley began to suck on her jewel, Cleopatra rolled her hips on the edge of the tub, dripping her juices down the front of Riley's chin and between her tits, bobbing in the rose-petal-covered water.

Holy fuck, Riley thought to herself. *Am I actually sucking the queen of Egypt's pussy?*

But Cleopatra's moans and shaking hips left little doubt this wasn't a dream and that the young college student had literally landed in the lap of the most famous and celebrated queen in history.

"My God," Cleopatra grunted, curling her fingers into Riley's hair. "That feels sublime. I might have to find a new role for you in the royal household if you keep licking me like that."

You have no idea, Riley grinned, raising her hand up to the queen's dripping slit and slipping two fingers inside her hole. Then she turned her palm upwards and curled her fingers forward, massaging her G-spot while rolling her tongue over the queen's burning clit in figure-8 patterns.

"Uhnnn," Cleopatra groaned, tilting her hips upward so she could watch Riley eat her pussy. "Right there. Don't stop. I'm going to come so hard on your pretty face."

"Mmm," Riley nodded, trilling her tongue more rapidly over the queen's engorged gland.

"Oh fuck," Cleopatra hissed, clasping Riley's face tightly between her flapping thighs. "Forgive me, but I feel the need to urinate. I can't stop it..."

"Yes, my queen," Riley murmured, knowing it wouldn't be urine the queen would release, but the special fluid in her Skene's Gland that had accumulated from the unique form of stimulation she'd been giving her. "Come all over my face."

Riley parted her fingers and pinched the queen's bulge, then pressed the tips hard against the roof of her pussy while circling her lips around her clit and sucking it hard into her mouth.

Suddenly, Cleopatra clamped her thighs tightly around her head and lurched forward, rocking her body over the edge of the tub while squirting her fluids over Riley's neck and shaking tits. It must have taken a full minute for her to stop shaking and groaning in the midst of the most powerful orgasm she'd ever experienced.

When she finally loosened her grip on Riley's head, she separated her legs, staring at the stream of liquid dripping down her bare chest.

"Oh dear," she said, placing her fingers under Riley's chin and lifting her face slowly. "I'm sorry, I don't know what came over me. I've never felt the urge to urinate while I was having sex before. Whatever you did to me unleashed a sensation I've never experienced–"

"It's not urine," Riley said, raising herself up out of the tub and standing before the queen with her breasts at face level. "Taste for yourself."

Cleopatra stared at Riley's dripping tits for a moment, then she leaned forward, licking her teats with the tip of her tongue. Then she sucked them hard into her mouth and moaned, nodding approvingly.

"See?" Riley smiled, enjoying the queen's attention on her sensitive tips. "It's only your natural feminine juices, which were emitted at the peak of sexual pleasure. The same juices that commingle with your partner's to facilitate procreation."

Cleopatra stared at Riley for a moment, wondering how such a young girl could be so knowledgeable about anatomy and physiology.

"Except none of my previous partners have made me come this way before," she said, peering up at Riley. "And I'm pretty sure I'd need a *different* kind of lubrication inside me to make babies."

"That's unfortunate," Riley said. "Because it's a singular pleasure when two women rub their bodies together to produce a similar effect."

"So *you* can do this too?" Cleopatra said, raising an eyebrow.

"When I'm with the right partner and receive the right kind of stimulation."

"Do I need to caress you with my fingers in the same manner?"

"Not always," Riley said. "If I'm properly aroused, it doesn't take much to make me ejaculate like a man. And I'm pretty damned turned on right now looking at the most beautiful woman in the world–"

"Lay down with me," Cleopatra said, spreading a towel on the tiles surrounding the tub and lying down face up. "Show me what else you can do."

"Are you sure you don't want to be the one on *top*?" Riley said. "I mean, you're the queen of Egypt after all..."

"I'm rather enjoying you being the one in charge for a change. Show me how two women make love where you come from. As long as I can watch you spray your juices the same way I just did."

Riley peered down at the queen's body lying on the floor and darted her eyes over her figure, contemplating the best position to share their mutual pleasure.

"Okay," she nodded. "As long as you don't mind getting a little twisted up."

"Twist away," Cleopatra smiled. "You can curl me up into a *pretzel* if it makes me come as hard as I did a few minutes ago."

Riley leaned down and slipped her fingers under Cleopatra's knees, then she pulled them up and bent them forward, pressing them up toward her pointed breasts. When the queen was hunched over in a crouched position, Riley placed her feet on opposite sides of her hips, then she slowly squatted down until her buttocks rested overtop of her upturned ass. When her pussy touched the queen's dripping slit, they both moaned, sliding their vulvas together while peering into one another's eyes.

Cleopatra glanced down at Riley's muff and smiled.

"I don't know how well I'll be able to see you squirt this way," she said. "Your bush is so thick, it's obscuring my line of sight to your folds."

"Don't worry," Riley grunted, rocking her pussy back and

forth over the queen's upturned ass. "You'll get a plenty good view from where you're sitting right now. But if you'd like me to stop and trim my locks so you can see more clearly, just give me the word–"

"Don't you dare," Cleopatra said, reaching forward to grab the sides of Riley's ass. "Maybe when we're finished, I can return the favor. I've never trimmed another woman's pubic hair before."

"I'd like that," Riley said, reaching down to intertwine her fingers with the queen's and lifting her hands to help maintain her balance perched atop her slippery buttocks.

She tilted her hips backwards a few degrees and when her clit touch Cleopatra's nub, they groaned, squeezing their hands harder together.

"Just when I thought it couldn't possibly get any better," the queen shuddered. "Your wet pussy feels even better on my shaved skin than your pretty *face* does."

"That makes two of us," Riley panted, beginning to feel her pleasure building toward a powerful climax.

"Are you getting close?" Cleopatra said. "Because I don't want to miss a moment of your display. I want to watch you spray your juices all over my pussy when you come."

"Yes," Riley rasped, squeezing the queen's hands until they turned white. "I'm almost there. Oh God, it's coming..."

"Show me," Cleopatra grunted, tilting her head and staring between their legs. "I'm coming too–"

Riley lifted her hips a few inches off Cleopatra's ass and tilted her hips forward, aiming her pussy toward her belly, then she squealed in pleasure as she jetted a powerful stream of juices forward along the queen's stomach. When it reached her pointed breasts, the stream shot upward, spraying a heavy rain down over her face while she blinked her eyes and licked her lips in delirious pleasure. Riley could feel the queen's hips shaking together with hers, and even though she didn't squirt her juices like she had the last time, there was little doubt she was experiencing another powerful climax while Riley stared at her puckering anus, convulsing in long, hard spasms.

"Fuck," Cleopatra groaned, watching Riley's pussy pulsing while she held her hands with shaking arms. "Squirt your juices all over my pussy. I can feel you dripping down the crease of my ass. I don't know how you got here, but now that you are, I never want to let you go. I can't wait to introduce you to my husband and see what surprises you can cook up with a throbbing *cock* added to the equation."

"I'll look forward to that," Riley shuddered, sitting back down atop Cleopatra's ass, still clasping her hands to keep from sliding off. "I'm already beginning to think about all the combinations and permutations..."

7

———

That evening, Riley could barely sleep, reliving her erotic encounter with Cleopatra, tossing and turning in her small cot next to the sleeping servant girl. The following morning, the queen sent word that Marc Antony was returning from a military campaign and that she wanted Riley to join them over dinner. Knowing there was a good chance she'd be invited back into Cleopatra's boudoir, she spent much of the day cleaning up and preparing for the event. The queen sent her a beautiful, low-cut silk dress and while it was being hand-tailored to cling to her slender figure, Iras helped prepare her hair. By the time the appointed hour for the event rolled around, Riley was tingling in excitement, eager to meet the queen's famous husband.

When she was escorted upstairs to the banquet hall, Riley gasped at the splendor of the room. Bedecked in billowing chiffon curtains and life-size bronze statues, the room glittered from the reflection of a giant crystal chandelier and a fifty-foot-long table festooned with shimmering silver platters, sparkling stemware, and huge floral arrangements. When she noticed the queen standing with a handsome man wearing a military uniform, Cleopatra motioned for her to join them.

She was wearing a long, off-the-shoulder, gold-lamé dress that highlighted all the curves of her beautiful figure and an enormous headdress with gold-embossed feathers and a gold crown. Riley was a little disappointed that the headdress covered the braid she'd worked so diligently to create earlier, but when the queen leaned in to kiss her on both cheeks, all of her other thoughts soon melted away.

"Riley," the queen said, stepping back to appraise her outfit. "You look gorgeous this evening. I'm so glad you could join us for our state dinner."

"Whatever my queen desires," Riley smiled, knowing she could hardly refuse the invitation.

Cleopatra turned toward the man standing next to her and extended her hand in his direction.

"I'd like to introduce you to my husband, Marc Antony. He's just returned from another successful military campaign, and this dinner is a celebration of his exploits."

Riley paused as she ran her eyes over his muscular figure, barely concealed by the metal chest plate outlining his carved pecs and the mid-thigh tunic exposing his powerful legs.

"Pleased to meet you, sir," she said, feeling weak at the knees while she curtsied. "I've heard so much about you. Is it true that you're descended from the Greek god, Hercules?"

"I don't know about that," Marc Antony chuckled. "But I sometimes feel like I've got the gods watching over me."

He glanced at Riley's tight-fitting gown, pausing a little longer to gaze at her deep cleavage.

"The queen has told me so much about you," he smiled.

"I'm looking forward to getting to know the newest member of our household."

"As am I," Riley said, feeling her pussy twitching while she stared at his broad shoulders.

Suddenly, two men wearing long white robes joined the group, bowing politely toward the queen.

"The conquering hero returns," one of them said, nodding toward Marc Antony.

"Just doing my part to protect the boundaries of the Roman Empire," Marc Antony said, bowing toward the man.

"Are you sure these conquests aren't for the benefit of *another* empire?" the man said, glancing toward Cleopatra with a strained smile.

"We're *partners* in these campaigns, are we not?" the queen said, glancing toward the other man. "While I provide the bulk of the funding, you provide protection from our common enemies."

"Partners," the man grunted. "I suppose that's *one* way of putting it."

Then he turned toward Riley and smiled.

"Who's this young lady by your side this evening? We haven't been properly introduced."

"My apologies," Cleopatra said, turning toward Riley. "This is my friend, Riley. She's visiting from Britannia. Riley, this is the Roman senator Octavian,and his consul, Marcus Lepidus."

"Britannia?" Octavian said, lifting an eyebrow. "Even our mighty Roman army hasn't forged that far afield. How did a young woman like you manage to make it all the way to Egypt?"

"It was a bit of a topsy-turvy journey," Riley said, trying to deflect the subject.

"I'm sure it was," Octavian said. "Perhaps our esteemed

general might enlist you as an advisor for his next campaign. He seems far more interested in conquering eastern territories than expanding our empire to the north."

"Perhaps I will," Marc Antony smiled. "I understand she's a woman of many talents."

"Come," Cleopatra said, eager to ease the nervous tension building between the group. "Why don't we stop talking politics for a moment and pause to enjoy a delicious dinner?"

While the dignitaries were seated at the large dining table, Riley racked her brain, trying to remember the role that Octavian and Marcus Lepidus had played in Roman history. The antipathy between them and Marc Antony was palpable, and it was obvious that whatever alliance they had formed, their oversize egos left little room for sharing the mantle of power. After the senators were seated opposite Cleopatra and Marc Antony at the center of the table, it suddenly came back to her.

After the Roman Emperor Julius Caesar was assassinated, the three statesmen had formed an uneasy partnership, with Octavian and Marcus Lepidus controlling the senate and Marc Antony placed in charge of the Roman Army. But as Caesar's nephew, Octavian had a claim to the throne, and with Marc Antony becoming ever more distracted with the Egyptian queen and conquering lands in the east, it was becoming apparent where his true allegiances lay.

When Cleopatra invited Riley to sit at her left side, the senators peered at her suspiciously, scowling at Marc Antony seated on her other side. While the servants poured wine and served the food, the two parties continued to make small talk, trying to disguise their obvious disdain for one another.

"What's your official title, Riley?" Octavian said, glancing toward the young girl. "Sitting in such a prominent position next to the queen, I imagine you have a very important role."

"Um–" Riley stammered, unsure how to reply.

"We're still deciding on her role," Cleopatra interrupted. "She has a unique perspective concerning geopolitics and an unusual knowledge of world history that belies her age."

"Is that so?" Octavian said, raising an eyebrow. "Please share your abundant wisdom. What do you believe will become of our two empires?"

Riley paused for a moment, mindful of the egos in the room and her responsibility not to alter the course of history.

"All empires eventually fall," she said. "But I believe the Roman Empire still has a few centuries of glory ahead of it."

"And what of the *Egyptian* empire?"

"That depends on how long the two parties can maintain a friendly alliance," Riley said, knowing full well that Octavian had no plans for sharing power with the wealthy queen. "With the riches of the Nile and the might of the Roman Army, the world is at your feet."

"Perhaps," Octavian nodded. "And what does history tell us about the prospects for sharing *control* between the two powerful dynasties?"

"Most men have an unquenchable thirst for power," Riley said, glancing toward Cleopatra. "Eventually, one gains the upper hand and eliminates the other."

"And what about *women*?" Octavian grinned. "Do they not have the same thirst for power?"

Suddenly, their conversation was interrupted by a young

child of roughly four years bursting into the room, squealing and running between the legs of the dining table.

"Caesarion!" Cleopatra yelled while her maids tried to scoop up the child. "You know better than to interrupt us when we're having company!"

The child emerged from under the table and clung to the queen's leg, and she leaned down to kiss him on the head before motioning for her attendants to take him away.

Caesarion, Riley thought to herself. *Caesar's son by Cleopatra, and the direct heir to the throne of Rome. So this places the timeline around 41 B.C.* She noticed Octavian sneering at the small child as it was led away before he returned his gaze toward Riley.

"You were saying?" he said.

"I was going to say that women have other priorities. I find they're more concerned about nurturing relationships and protecting their families than conquering new territories."

"Yes," Octavian nodded, peering at Cleopatra with thin eyes. "Their loyalties are always first and foremost with their *children.*"

8

After dinner, Cleopatra and Marc Antony bade farewell to their houseguests, who said they had to return to Rome on urgent business. Marc Antony was still fuming about Octavian's thinly veiled threats, and they retired to the terrace overlooking the Mediterranean Sea with Riley for after-dinner drinks.

"That pompous ass," he said, gulping down a heavy swig of sherry. "Did you hear how many times he insulted us?"

"I'm not sure they were insults so much as innuendo," Cleopatra said, clasping his hand gently.

"Ridiculing my triumphs in the east and suggesting Riley as my new military advisor. And the way he sneered at you and me over dinner. It's like he's already declared himself the new emperor."

"He doesn't have enough support in the Senate to consolidate power," Cleopatra said. "You still have many allies on your side."

Marc Antony peered out over the darkening sea, watching Octavian's escort vessels trailing off into the distance.

"If they can conspire to overthrow Caesar, they can easily swing the votes to his favor. And with me being away fighting their wars, my voice is slowly losing its influence."

"Perhaps you should go back to reestablish your status, at least for a short time. Remind them who's keeping the barbarians from the gate. I'll be fine here on my own for a little while."

"That's the problem," Marc Antony said, peering toward Riley. "After you told me about your little affair with our new houseguest, I'm not sure I can trust you to keep the candle burning."

"Oh, come now," Cleopatra said, smiling at Riley. "You know there's no substitute for your big cock. Why don't we all go to bed and share the spoils *together*? I think you might find our houseguest is more resourceful than her youthful demeanor might suggest."

Marc Antony paused for a moment, cocking his head in Riley's direction.

"I know how much you enjoy the affections of other women," Cleopatra said, grabbing both of their hands and pulling them in the direction of her boudoir. "Let's celebrate your latest conquest with a *double* dose of attention. What do you say, Riley–are you up for a little more fun?"

"I'm game if you are," Riley smiled, noticing the front of Marc Antony's tunic tenting outward.

When they reached the queen's boudoir, Cleopatra pushed Marc Antony down onto the large four-poster bed and began unbuttoning his clothes. When he was naked, she pulled off her dress and kneeled over his face, dangling her bare pussy inches away from his bulging eyes.

"What's *this?*" he said, peering up at her newly shaved mound.

She pulled off her headdress and placed it on the bed beside her pillow.

"I told you Riley was a woman of many talents. After she finished styling my hair, I asked if she wouldn't mind trimming me down below."

"I'd say she did a little more than just a *trim*," Marc Antony said, his thick penis beginning to rise and expand while Riley looked on quietly behind them.

"Don't you like it?" Cleopatra smiled. "I thought you'd enjoy kissing my peachka without all those scratchy hairs getting in the way."

"Mmm," Antony nodded, grabbing the queen's ass and pulling her wet pussy down over his face.

"I knew you'd approve," Cleopatra groaned as he swirled his tongue over her bulging clit.

She turned her head around and noticed Riley staring at the two of them like a deer caught in the headlights.

"Are you just going to stand there and *watch*?" the queen said. "Feel free to join in any time. That is, if you enjoy playing with *men* as much as you do women."

"Oh, I like men well enough," Riley nodded, pulling off her dress and throwing it over the back of an empty chair. "Especially one as well-endowed as this one."

She walked up to the foot of the bed and leaned over, engulfing Marc Antony's huge hard-on as far as she could in her watering mouth. He groaned when he felt her lips on his tool, spreading his legs further apart and raising his feet to the edge of the bed. Riley placed one hand around his balls and grasped his shaft with the other, stroking his long organ while she expertly sucked and trilled the edge of his frenulum with her swirling tongue. He began grunting and rocking his hips, and the queen glanced behind her back, nodding approvingly.

"I like seeing your cock in another girl's mouth," she said. "Especially one as pretty and skilled as this one. But don't take him all the way, Riley. I have other plans for that magnificent organ. We don't want him to spend all of his energy before we've both had a chance to fully enjoy his weapon."

"Mmm," Riley nodded, beginning to feel Marc Antony's balls rising in mounting pleasure. She pulled her mouth off his pole, and it fluttered over his stomach, emitting a drop of precum and sliding down the side of his shaft.

Cleopatra peered down at Riley's pussy, noticing that she'd shaven it bare like her own, and smiled.

"What do you think, sweetheart?" she said, turning back toward Marc Antony. "How'd you like to suck *two* shaved pussies at the same time?"

When his eyes widened in excitement, Cleopatra motioned for Riley to join her at the head of the bed. She climbed up on the mattress and the two women faced one another, interlocking their tongues while they pressed their mounds together over Marc Antony's bulging eyes. While they ground their pussies together, they slowly lowered their hips over Marc Antony's face until they smothered him with their dripping vulvas. He lapped their bare snatches with his tongue and they moaned excitedly into each other's mouths.

"Fuck, that feels good," Cleopatra panted, gazing at Riley. "Are you ready to show my husband our *other* surprise?"

"You mean–?"

"Absolutely," Cleopatra nodded. "We said we were going

to shower him with affection. I don't think we should hold anything back."

"Mmm," Riley groaned, feeling her pleasure quickly approaching the tipping point. "Are you sure? This could get a bit messy..."

"We *like* messy, don't we dear?" Cleopatra said, peering down at Marc Antony's dripping face.

"Ungh," he grunted, unable to speak with two grinding pussies covering his mouth.

Cleopatra and Riley tilted their hips closer together, and when their clits touched, Riley threw her head back, releasing all the pent-up pressure building around her hips. When she started jetting her juices over Marc Antony's face and Cleopatra's pussy, he flinched, unsure at first what was happening. But when his wife began squirting shortly after, he grabbed both of their asses, pulling them down hard over his face while he slurped up their juices like a famished animal. When they finally stopped cumming, the two women slumped down on opposite sides of Marc Antony, smiling at his flushed, dripping face.

"What do you think, my love?" Cleopatra said. "Was that a suitable prize for the homecoming hero?"

"It was certainly an *unexpected* one," he panted. "What other surprises have you two cooked up while I was away?"

"We were saving the best one for last," Cleopatra smiled, noticing his turgid cock still flapping excitedly over his stomach. "It's time to show you what two shaved pussies feel when there's a throbbing dick placed between them."

Riley glanced at the queen and nodded, happy to get a piece of Marc Antony's oversize cock any way she could have it.

Cleopatra raised up on her knees, then turned around to straddle his stomach, facing toward his feet.

"Mmm," she said, dragging her hips toward Marc Antony's upright organ. "Let's see if we can create a *three-way* fountain this time, Riley. Let's give him a pussy sandwich he'll never forget."

Riley nodded and crawled down to the other end of the bed, kneeling over Marc Antony's balls, facing the queen. She placed her arms around her back and pulled herself forward, clamping Marc Antony's pole between their pussies. When they began to raise and lower their hips together, he groaned, grabbing the back of Cleopatra's ass.

"Yes," he panted. "Stroke my dick with your beautiful bare pussies. This feels like I've died and gone to heaven."

"Not quite yet, my love," Cleopatra said. "Not until we're finished with you. We're just getting started."

"Mhhh," Riley groaned, dragging her clit up and down Marc Antony's throbbing pole. "I'm not so sure about that. I don't know how much longer I can last like this. I'm about to experience my own kind of nirvana any moment now."

"Let it go baby," Cleopatra nodded, wrapping her arms around Riley's back and pressing their tits together. "I'm going to cum soon too."

The feeling of the queen's firm tits rubbing against hers and Marc Antony's burning tool flexing between their pussies was too much for Riley to resist. While she watched a flush slowly spreading over his chest and up over his neck, she began convulsing over his balls, jetting one powerful stream of liquid after another over his purple prick and Cleopatra's bare cunt. Within seconds, Marc Antony growled, digging his fingertips into the side of Cleopatra's ass, squirting thick ropes of cum up over their bellies and under their breasts. When Cleopatra felt her husband coming between their rocking hips, she joined the others in a symphony of moans, holding tightly onto Riley while the three of them thrashed and shook their hips together in unison.

When they finally finished coming, Riley flopped down onto the bed, dripping from a mixture of Marc Antony's cum, the queen's juices, and her own sweat.

I suppose that's one way to experience a Roman bath, she smiled to herself. *Who knew the famous queen was so kinky? To hell with walking like an Egyptian, those ancient inscriptions should show how they fucked like one.*

9

The next morning, Cleopatra and Marc Antony invited Riley to join them for breakfast on the terrace, where they continued their discussion of how to address Octavian's mounting hostility.

"You seem to have an unusual perspective on the situation here in the Middle East," Marc Antony said to Riley, taking a sip of his mimosa. "What do you think Octavian and Marcus Lepidus's next move will be?"

Riley paused as she peered out over the glimmering Mediterranean Sea, watching the sun rise from the east. She knew from her history books that it wouldn't take long for the ambitious senator to consolidate his power in Rome and send an armada to overthrow Cleopatra's government. But she'd have to choose her words carefully to not reveal her knowledge of the future while still maintaining the two lovers' trust.

"It's not Marcus Lepidus you have to worry about," she said. "It's obvious that Octavian speaks for both of them. His comments over dinner last night left little doubt that he has no interest in maintaining this fragile alliance much longer."

"But he's only one voice in the Senate," Marc Antony said. "We still have many friends who will stand by our side."

"I'm concerned they will only stand by your side so long as they believe you can continue to protect them."

"But I'm the commander of the army. Surely he wouldn't try to seize power with twenty-five legions under my control?"

"Your army is spread over a wide area of Europe and the Middle East. Octavian controls the bulk of the naval fleet positioned near Rome. They could cross the Mediterranean before your army had a chance to mobilize."

Cleopatra leaned forward, narrowing her eyes angrily at the idea Rome would invade her territory.

"We have our *own* navy to protect Egypt," she said.

"But the Roman fleet is a well-paid, professional force with considerably more experience. I'm afraid your navy would be no match for his if it came down to a direct confrontation."

"She has a point," Marc Antony said, leaning back in his chair while he peered at Riley thoughtfully. "How do you think we can resist this aggression?"

Riley hesitated as her eyes darted over the sea in the direction of Italy. She remembered how Marc Antony returned to Rome in 40 B.C. and married Octavian's sister in an effort to ease tensions, only to return to Cleopatra three years later to make a final stand against his superior forces.

"I'm afraid the queen was accurate in suggesting the only way to safeguard your position is to return to Rome, where you can keep a closer watch over Octavian and continue building alliances in the Senate."

"And if I don't?" Marc Antony said.

"Then it's only a matter of time before Octavian makes

his move and sends the Roman fleet to take back what he considers rightfully his."

A fter their discussion with Riley, Cleopatra and Marc Antony decided to convene a war council with their military chiefs to discuss the defense of Alexandria. Marc Antony was reticent to leave the queen alone when Octavian could launch a naval attack at any moment, and he invited Riley to the meeting for her continued insight. Although she was only eighteen years of age, her knowledge of military affairs and strategy had already made her a valuable asset to the besieged couple.

"Thank you for coming to this impromptu meeting," the queen said, addressing the collection of senior officers hunched around a large table carrying a map of the Mediterranean. "I've asked you here to discuss a matter of growing urgency. It has recently come to our attention that Rome may be making plans to invade Egypt."

"Rome?" one of the Egyptian generals said, peering at Marc Antony with a furrowed brow. "I thought they were our allies?"

"Only *some* of them, it appears," Marc Antony said.

"We believe Octavian may be mobilizing his naval fleet for an assault on Alexandria," Cleopatra continued. "I'd like to develop plans for repelling his force if it comes down to it."

One of the admirals pointed toward a small collection of miniature ships positioned in Alexandria harbor, then a much larger fleet stationed at Misenum in the Tyrrhenian Sea.

"Our smaller galleys are no match for the Roman

warships," he said. "With their superior speed and displacement, they would tear us apart in hours."

"What about your catapults?" Marc Antony said. "Can't we sink them before they reach our shores?"

"Possibly," the admiral said. "But even mounted on the highest promontory, their range out to sea is only about five hundred meters. A Roman quinquereme can close that gap in a matter of minutes. They'd be upon us before we had time to reload."

"What about our army?" Cleopatra said.

"We've been reliant up until now on the Roman army for most of our protection," the top general said. "With three hundred soldiers on each ship and over one hundred vessels, their force of thirty thousand soldiers would quickly overwhelm our much smaller army."

"Can't you move some of your men from the nearby territories?" Cleopatra said, turning toward Marc Antony.

"Maybe," he said. "But the closest ones are in Syria and Judea. It would take *weeks* to move that many men to Alexandria."

"So, you're telling me we're at the mercy of the Roman navy, with no way to defend ourselves?" Cleopatra said, shaking her head.

Suddenly, Riley stepped forward, picking up a miniature model positioned on one of the hills overlooking the capital.

"Are these what your catapults look like?" she said.

The Egyptian generals glared at the young girl, incensed that she had the temerity to interrupt their important deliberations.

"Yes," one of them said. "What of it?"

"This is a fairly primitive design," Riley said, turning the model around slowly in her hands. "I can help you build one with five times the throwing power and distance. If we can build enough of them fast enough, we might be able to sink enough of their ships to even the scales."

"We?" the general said. "Who is this child who pretends to know more about military strategy than our experienced generals?"

"Just hear her out for a minute," Cleopatra nodded. "She comes from another land where they may have more advanced technology. Riley, how do you know about this special weapon?"

Riley paused for a moment, knowing she couldn't tell the group she'd come from the future, and that as an engineering student at MIT, she had advanced knowledge of physics and mechanics.

"I've seen a different version of these using a longer arm balanced on an off-center fulcrum. It's fairly easy to build, and we could put together a working prototype in a matter of days."

Cleopatra paused as she peered around the table at the military planners staring at Riley like she was from another planet.

"Well, I don't see any bright ideas coming from the other side of the table," she said. "I want you men to give this young lady whatever resources she needs to build this special weapon. If it turns out to be as effective as she suggests, we might owe our lives to this mere child."

10

───────

For the next few days, Riley supervised the construction of a new, more advanced catapult. When it was finished and the generals tested it atop a cliff overlooking Alexandria, everybody was amazed how much further it could throw a heavy projectile out to sea. The queen immediately authorized the construction of ten more pieces, and while the work continued, Marc Antony supervised the training of operators shooting targets placed at varying distances in the bay.

When everyone was satisfied they knew how to operate the devices, a twenty-four-hour watch was placed atop the promontory. Within a matter of days, one of the lookouts announced a line of advancing warships in the distance, and Marc Antony and Cleopatra scurried atop the hill to monitor the invasion. As the armada sailed ever-closer to shore, Cleopatra's eyes widened, alarmed by the number of ships Octavian had mobilized.

"There must be over a *hundred* of them," she said, turning toward Marc Antony with a frightened look. "Are you sure these weapons will be able to stop that many ships?"

"Their first mistake was to bunch up their fleet into one large mass," he nodded. "He's hoping this show of force will increase the chance of us surrendering. But it just makes it easier for us to strike them more quickly."

He turned toward the catapult operators and nodded, raising his sword.

"Prepare to fire on my signal," he said.

While the flotilla sailed closer to shore, the Egyptian soldiers' eyes widened, watching the sheer number of oars swinging together in unison.

"Shouldn't we shoot them while we have them in our sights?" Cleopatra said. "I thought these catapults could fire that far out to sea."

"We're only going to have one chance at this," Marc Antony nodded, holding his sword steadily over his head. "If we strike too early and miss, they'll scatter their boats and it will be harder to thin their ranks. We just have to wait another minute or so..."

While the seconds ticked by in slow motion, the catapult operators' hands quivered over the release mechanisms, eager to fire the heavy stones dangling from a long sling attached to the main hurling arm. When Marc Antony finally swept his sword down, the arms swung forward in unison, hurling the giant rocks high into the air and arcing over the flotilla. When they landed with a loud crash, pulverizing many of the boats, the fleet began to separate, trying to evade the unexpected volley of missiles.

"Reload!" Marc Antony shouted, glaring at the catapult operators. "Don't give them a chance to disperse. We need to strike while they're still vulnerable!"

While another team raised a new round of rocks into the

pouches, the catapult operators spun the winch handles around, rapidly retracting the hurling arms. Then they readjusted the stopping position of the arm and turned the frames in the direction of the scattering ships, releasing a new volley of stones, sinking five more vessels. By the time they fired their third round, the remaining ships began to turn around, fleeing back in the direction of Rome. A loud cheer spread over the hill, with the soldiers and generals congratulating one another on their victory.

"I wouldn't have believed it if I hadn't seen it with my own eyes," Cleopatra nodded, breathing a sigh of relief while she hugged Riley tightly. "It looks like your brilliant invention saved the day."

But while everyone was hugging and cheering, Marc Antony peered solemnly out to sea at the retreating band of ships.

"We may have won this battle," he said. "But I'm afraid the war has only started. Octavian sent only half of his fleet to attack us, and the next time he won't be so careless with mounting a frontal assault. They can just as easily land their ships on our flanks and advance their troops over land. We'll have to come up with a new strategy to repel their next attack, which will almost surely be much larger."

That night, Cleopatra, Marc Antony, and Riley had a more subdued discussion on the terrace, peering out over the quiet sea as it shimmered with the reflection of a full moon.

"I don't suppose you've got another idea for stopping an entire *army*?" Cleopatra said, glancing at Riley while she sipped her tea.

"Not one that can be built with present-day materials," she said, knowing that gunpowder still wouldn't be invented for hundreds of centuries. "I'm afraid the next battle will have to be fought the old-fashioned way, with swords and arrows and soldiers on the ground."

Cleopatra wrinkled her forehead then peered over in the direction of Marc Antony.

"Have you begun to move your troops from the east?" she said to her pensive husband.

"My generals tell me they should begin arriving in the capital within two or three days," he nodded.

"Do you think it will be enough to repel Octavian's forces?"

"That depends on how many men he can muster and how quickly he can reassemble the navy," Marc Antony said. "I'm afraid we're going to find out sooner than we expected how much support he's built in the Senate."

<hr>

That night, Riley returned to her quarters, unable to sleep, already knowing the outcome of the upcoming battle. She knew that while Marc Antony had been absent from Rome, Octavian had been busy purging his allies from the Senate and reestablishing ties with the generals, impatient at Marc Antony's increasing distraction with the queen instead of conquering new territories. Her only hope was to try to persuade Marc Antony and Cleopatra to agree to Octavian's terms or flee for their safety. As much as it pained her to change the course of history, she'd grown far too close to her new lovers to watch them die an ignominious death.

11

The next morning, Marc Antony convened another meeting with his war council while Cleopatra and Riley shared a quiet breakfast on the terrace. It was a bright and sunny day, and as Riley peered out over the glimmering Mediterranean from the tall ramparts of the palace, it was hard to imagine the magnificent city would soon lie submerged in rubble under the sea.

"Did you sleep well last night?" Cleopatra said, sipping her tea.

"Not really," Riley said. "I was too worried about the outcome of the next battle."

"But Marc Antony is still in charge of the army," the queen said. "When they arrive in Alexandria, we'll have a much larger force than Octavian can mobilize with his weakened navy."

"Perhaps," Riley said. "But that assumes his generals will remain faithful to the chain of command. We've seen before how fickle the loyalties of senior officers can be. If they can overthrow Caesar, they can overthrow anybody."

"What else can we do?" Cleopatra said, pinching her

eyebrows in dismay. "We're surrounded on both sides by the army. It's not like we have anywhere to run."

"You're the richest woman in the Mediterranean. You still have enough time to slip away. You could load up one of your ships with gold and sail to Morocco and live out the rest of your days in relative peace and comfort."

"Morocco?"

"To the west," Riley pointed, realizing many of the countries of North Africa still had to be named. "Through the Strait of Gibraltar. There's only so far the Roman Army can be stretched. You and Marc Antony would be safe if you kept a low profile."

"And give up this kingdom that has survived the better part of three centuries?"

"All kingdoms eventually fall," Riley said. "Unfortunately, right now, Rome is at the peak of its power and Egypt is on the decline. But it's not too late to save your life. You're the most famous woman who ever lived. There's no reason why your legacy has to end in infamy."

Cleopatra paused while she peered pensively out to sea.

"You seem to know an awful lot about history for such a young girl," she said.

"I've traveled and seen more than you can imagine," Riley said. "Trust me when I say there's only two ways this can end. With Alexandria up in flames or with you and Marc Antony safely stolen away."

"What about you?" the queen said. "What will you do?"

"I'm not the one Octavian fears. I can move about freely without a price on my head."

"Where would you go?" Cleopatra said. "It might not be so easy for you to sail back to Britannia once Octavian controls all the sea lanes."

"You're not the *only* one with resources," Riley smiled. "I have my own method of stealing away."

"Will you come with me and Marc Antony?"

"The two of you have a special place in history. You'll have famous stories created by the leading writers and playwrights. I don't belong in these stories."

Cleopatra gazed at Riley for a long moment, then her attention was diverted by Marc Antony, who walked out onto the terrace and sat down solemnly beside her.

"Any word from your generals?" she said, noticing the deep lines etched in his forehead.

"They've been strangely silent for the past two days," he said, furrowing his brows.

"What do you think it means?"

"I'm not sure. It's possible the couriers were intercepted. But I'm growing more worried by the moment."

"What about the *Egyptian* army?" the queen said. "Are they prepared to fight alone if it comes down to it?"

"There is no question of their loyalty to the queen," he nodded. "But they are ten thousand men facing an army potentially ten times that size."

"What about the catapults?" Cleopatra said. "Can't we build more of them to repel the invading army?"

"A few stones won't stop a hundred thousand men. I'm afraid if we don't receive reinforcements soon, they will quickly overrun our positions."

Cleopatra paused for a moment then she glanced toward Riley.

"Maybe it's time we acquiesced to Octavian's demands," she said. "Perhaps he'll allow us to stay on as governors of the state. I still have considerable influence and authority in the region."

"After we sunk twenty of his galleys?" Marc Antony said. "I think that ship has already sailed. He'd be more likely to parade us in chains in his victory procession or put our heads on a pike."

"We can still steal away somewhere safe," Cleopatra said. "What if we took our ships to the other side of the Mediterranean and rebuilt our army? Maybe we could marshal support from the indigenous people and mount a new offensive..."

"A wild band of savages wielding sticks against a huge professional army? No, we either stand and fight together, or lose with honor."

Cleopatra's eyes welled up with tears as she reached out to clasp Marc Antony's hand.

"But there's still a chance to save ourselves," she said. "With our combined wealth, we could find another place to settle down, far away from the Roman sphere of influence."

"And run away like *cowards*?" Marc Antony said, tightening the muscles in his jaw. "The queen of Egypt and the supreme commander of the Roman Army?"

"Those are just titles," Cleopatra said. "We could still live like kings far away from all this madness."

"And what would history make of us then?"

"We've already created our own legacy," Cleopatra said, squeezing Marc Antony's hand. "Like Riley said, all empires eventually fall. But there's no reason *our* history has to end like this. Let's save ourselves to fight another day."

Marc Antony paused while he peered out to sea, shaking his head pensively.

"We still have a little more time to think," Cleopatra said, nodding toward Riley. "Let's at least enjoy the remaining moments of solitude we have together. Why don't we take a break from all this war planning and pause to enjoy the simple pleasures of life? I've still got a few stories I want to tell..."

12

Cleopatra led Riley and Marc Antony back to her bedroom, where the trio made love for the rest of the night. But at dawn, there was a loud rap on her door, where one of her aides announced the arrival of the Roman Army, closing in from both sides of the city. Marc Antony leapt out of bed and pulled on his military uniform, breathing a sigh of relief.

"Thank heavens," he said. "It's finally time to show Octavian who's really in charge around here."

"Wait," Cleopatra said, reaching out to grab his hand as he headed toward the door. "What if they're no longer on our side? What if he's turned them against us?"

"Then we'll fight to the death defending what is rightfully ours. The Egyptian empire has stood far longer than Rome, and its glory days are far from over."

Cleopatra peered at Marc Antony with a frightened expression, then she flung her arms around his shoulders.

"Just promise me one thing," she said. "If the battle turns in their favor, come to me so we can be together. I don't want you to be captured and paraded as Octavian's prize."

"I will try, my love," Marc Antony said. "But if I'm not able, I want you and Riley to escape while you still can. I'll hold them off as long as I can."

"Be careful, darling," Cleopatra said, giving Marc Antony a long kiss. "I will await your return."

When Marc Antony left the bedroom, Riley and Cleopatra got dressed and repaired to the terrace so they could watch the developments from high ground. When they emerged onto the balcony, they saw two large masses of soldiers waiting outside the city gates while Octavian's navy closed in from the north.

"My God," Cleopatra said, staring at the spectacle. "There must be a hundred thousand soldiers between their combined forces."

"Do you think the army will still be loyal to Marc Antony?" Riley said.

"I think we're about to find out," the queen said, watching three horses galloping toward the eastern gate of the city. When they reached the gate, the doors swung open and Marc Antony's horse trotted out slowly to greet the troops. There was a long pause while the two senior commanders commiserated, then Marc Antony's horse turned around and retreated back through the gate, with the doors closing behind him.

"What does that mean?" Riley said, watching the scene in rapt attention.

"It means Marc Antony's no longer in control of the Roman Army," Cleopatra said, shaking her head.

A few moments later, the sound of loud horns trumpeted on both sides of the city gates then a battering ram broke through the entrance, followed by a stream of soldiers running in the direction of the palace. The catapults began hailing down huge stones atop the invading horde, but it barely seemed to slow them down. When the queen's soldiers met the two sides head on, there was a loud clang of metal and shields, while Marc Antony and the Egyptian generals retreated further and further into the courtyard.

Riley watched the battle for a brief moment, then she turned toward Cleopatra.

"I don't think your forces will be able to resist them much longer," she said. "If you want to escape, you'll need to do so soon."

Cleopatra peered down into the courtyard, watching Marc Antony fighting valiantly while Octavian's troops closed in from three sides.

"I can't leave my husband," she cried. "He promised that he'd return to me."

"All of his escape routes appear to be closed off," Riley said, noticing the swarm closing in around him. "He'd want you to save yourself."

Cleopatra's eyes welled up with tears, then she scribbled a note on a piece of parchment, motioning for her trusted servant, Iras.

"Give this to the palace guards and see if they can take it to Marc Antony," she said, handing her the note. "But hurry— we don't have much time."

"Yes, my queen," Iras said, rushing off in the direction of the turmoil.

Riley peered at Cleopatra, pinching her eyebrows.

"What did you say to him?" she said.

"I told him I'd taken the poison of an asp, unwilling to see him taken from me. I can't bear to see him captured and humiliated. I'm hoping that he'll take his own life before it's too late."

Riley watched while one of the guards broke through the fighting, handing Marc Antony the queen's note. He paused for a moment to read it, then he kneeled in the sand, turning in the direction of the palace balcony. He removed a small knife from his belt and peered up, thrusting the blade into the side of his chest. When he collapsed onto the ground, his aides picked him up and dragged him toward the palace doors, barricading it behind them.

"What have I done?" Cleopatra suddenly screamed. "I've killed the only man I truly loved. Oh, my dear, sweet Marc Antony..."

Riley wrapped her arms around the queen, trying to console her while she wept on her shoulder.

"You saved him from a far worse fate," she said. "Your love will live on for eternity. But if you want to save yourself, you have to leave now. The Romans will be at the palace doors any moment now."

"I can't even *walk* right now," Cleopatra said, overcome by grief. "I don't want to go anywhere without my husband. I'm nothing without him."

Suddenly, there was a loud clamor as a group of Egyptian soldiers dragged the bleeding Marc Antony through the anteroom toward the queen's balcony. His head was bobbing limply, but his feet were still moving while his aides pulled him toward Cleopatra.

"You're alive!" she said, rushing toward him with outstretched arms.

"As are you," Marc Antony said weakly.

"Oh, my brave soldier," she said, holding him as he collapsed into her arms. "I knew you wouldn't surrender so long as you thought I was alive. I thought this was the only way–"

"It's alright," he panted, struggling to breathe. "I'm happy you're still alive. There's still time to save yourself. Use the secret passageway. My aides will protect you until you reach the river. If you disguise yourself, you should be able to escape inland. I love you and always will..."

Then Marc Antony coughed up some blood and breathed one long, last heavy sigh, closing his eyes as he collapsed onto the queen's shoulder.

"Nooo!" Cleopatra wailed. "You can't leave me! I won't go without you!"

"My queen," one of the palace guards said, listening to the sound of loud pounding coming from the palace's front door. "You must leave now if you hope to save yourself."

"I can't, I can't!" Cleopatra said, leaning over Marc Antony's motionless body. "I won't leave without him. Octavian will put his body on display for the whole world to see."

Riley glanced up at the guard, desperate to find a way out of their predicament.

"Would it be possible to bring his body *with* us?" she said.

"I think so," he nodded. "But we only have a few seconds before the soldiers will break into the palace."

"Where is this secret passageway? Riley said, glancing at the queen.

"Downstairs, near the servant quarters," she said.

"Come on," Riley said, lifting her up and threading her arm around her waist. "We haven't any time to lose."

"Bring him," Cleopatra said, nodding toward the guards.

As the group scurried down the stairs and past the bulging front door, Cleopatra led them through a labyrinth of winding hallways toward a brass door with an engraving of her royal seal. While she fished a heavy key into the lock, Riley turned toward the queen, suddenly remembering her time machine.

"You go ahead, I'll join you in a few moments," she said.

"What could you possibly need at a moment like this?" Cleopatra said, shaking her head.

"Something that guarantees our safety," Riley smiled. "If I'm not back before the soldiers arrive, you go on without me."

"Okay, but hurry," Cleopatra said, reaching out to squeeze Riley's hand. "I don't want to lose both of you."

"Don't worry," Riley nodded. "I promise that I'll live to fight another day."

While she raced down the corridor in the direction of her sleeping quarters, Riley shook her head, hardly believing that she'd found herself in the middle of one of the most dramatic historical events of all time.

It's not over yet, she thought to herself, swinging open her bedroom door and grabbing her time machine hidden atop the armoire. *There's still time to rewrite at least one part of history...*

13

———

When Riley returned to the secret passageway, the queen motioned for her to hurry, hearing the sounds of soldiers clamoring down the palace stairs. After they closed the heavy door, a group of guards stayed behind to slow their advance while Cleopatra and Riley rushed down a narrow corridor toward a waiting fishing boat moored at the side of the Nile.

"Come," she said to Riley, motioning for the boat's captain to set off upstream. "This should provide some cover for us while we slip away from the action."

While they watched the last gasp of resistance fizzle out as the Roman soldiers swarmed into the palace and seized the catapults, they held on to each other, trembling in shock.

"What an inglorious ending to one of the greatest civilizations of all time," the queen said, a tear running down her cheek. "Alexander the Great and my forefathers must be rolling over in their grave."

"Don't worry," Riley said, squeezing her hand. "Your

legacy and that of Alexandria will live on for centuries to come."

Cleopatra turned her head to peer at the lifeless body of Marc Antony lying next to her under the gunwales.

"Unfortunately, the glory days of my husband have also come to an end."

"You shared a love for the ages," Riley nodded. "That too will live on long after you've both left this earth."

"We'll have to see about that," Cleopatra said, glancing up at the billowing columns of smoke rising above Alexandria as their boat slowly sailed upriver.

"So what happens now?" Riley said. "Where will you go?"

"I'm not sure," Cleopatra said, shaking her head. "This river is over four thousand miles long. Right now, I just want to put as much distance between me and Octavian as possible."

Riley nodded, noticing the queen escaped with barely her nightgown on her back.

"It's too bad you weren't able to carry some of your treasure with you in the mad dash to escape," she said. "You would have been able to live out the rest of your days in peace and comfort with the fortune you built."

Cleopatra paused for a moment, then she motioned for Riley to join her below deck.

"Come," she said. "I want to show you something."

When they reached the bottom of the steps, Riley's eyes flared open when she saw a huge pile of gleaming gold coins and artifacts lying on the floor of the galley.

"What the...?" she said. "How–"

"I wanted to be ready, just in case," Cleopatra said. "There was something about the delay in the arrival of the Roman troops that I found suspicious. I had my staff load up the ship last night in case we needed to make a hasty exit."

"That was a brilliant masterstroke," Riley nodded, noticing the queen's golden headdress resting on the side of the pile. "You even managed to save your crown."

"You never know when it might come in handy," the queen smiled, placing the headdress atop her head. "Who knows, maybe I'll make a triumphant return to Alexandria someday."

"If anyone can do it, it would surely be you," Riley said.

Later that day, the fishing boat paused at the side of the riverbank to bury Marc Antony's remains. Cleopatra wanted his headstone to announce his name and exploits, but Riley suggested that if she wanted his grave to remain undisturbed, it would be better to leave it unmarked. She remembered from her history books that neither his nor the queen's grave were ever found, and knowing modern civilization's penchant for digging up ancient crypts, she knew this was the best way to protect their legacy.

That night, the two women retired to their cabin to discuss future plans.

"You mentioned Mesopotamia," Cleopatra said, sitting cross-legged on the bed, facing toward Riley. "Why do you think this is such a good place for me to flee?"

"It's far enough from the Roman outposts to keep you out of sight," Riley said. "And it's one of the few places outside Rome with an urban civilization and advanced culture. I think you'll find it quite comfortable there."

Cleopatra squinted her eyes, shaking her head at Riley.

"How could you possibly know so much about this

place? It's not so easily reachable by sea. You're far too young to have such worldly knowledge."

Riley paused for a long moment, then she nodded her head slowly.

"Can you keep a secret?"

"I think we've shared enough confidences for you to know you can trust me," Cleopatra smiled.

Riley pulled her small smartphone-shaped time machine out of her pocket and handed it to the queen.

"I didn't really come here by ship," she said. "And I'm not from Britannia, at least not directly. This device is a time machine. I came here from another time, far into the future."

"A time machine?" Cleopatra said, turning the glass and metal device over in her hands. "How does it work?"

"If you tap the surface, a funnel appears that pulls you into another dimension. Why don't we go *together* this time? We could have an adventure like Thelma and Louise."

"Thelma and who?"

"They're two female adventurers from my time," Riley smiled.

"And how did it end for them?" Cleopatra said.

"Not so well, actually," Riley frowned. "But then again, they didn't have this magic device to help them get out of a tight spot..."

"I don't know," Cleopatra said, snuggling closer to Riley. "I've grown pretty comfortable living in my own time. But now that you mention it, I do like the idea about getting into some tight spots..."

She untied Riley's silk robe, then lifted both of their nightgowns over their heads, leaning forward to press their breasts together while the two women kissed softly.

"Why don't you stay with me a little longer?" she said,

mashing her moist pussy against Riley's. "We've got enough money for *both* of us to live like queens. I could use your wise counsel to keep me out of trouble, plus I'll miss your special hairdressing skills."

"Mmm," Riley hummed, wrapping her arms around Cleopatra's back while they ground their pussies together. "It's tempting, but I'll eventually have to get back to where I came from. There will be other people missing me."

"Other *lovers*?"

"No," Riley said. "Friends, parents, colleagues. I've got my *own* life on the other side of the world."

"I'm sure they won't miss you for another couple of hours," Cleopatra grunted, rolling her hips against Riley's while their juices dripped down the cracks of their asses.

"No," Riley groaned, feeling their clits pressing together. "I don't imagine they will."

"Oh, Riley," the queen moaned. "I'm going to miss you. I can't thank you enough for what you've done and how you saved me–"

"I'm just sorry I couldn't save your husband too," Riley said, kissing Cleopatra's neck softly. "My time machine only gives me so much power."

"You can't stop an entire army," Cleopatra said. "Like you said, empires are destined to rise and fall. It just wasn't our time."

"If you only knew how much longer your names will live on," Riley said. "Octavian's name will soon be forgotten, but yours and Marc Antony's will live on forever."

"I'm glad," Cleopatra smiled. "But right now, there's only *one* memory I want to hold dear. I want to remember the feeling of you squirting all over my pussy when we climax together."

"Oh, Cleopatra," Riley groaned. "Yes, my queen, *come with me.*"

After Riley and Cleopatra finished making love, the queen fell asleep and Riley crept out of the bedroom, removing her time machine from her pocket. While she held her trembling hand over the screen, she peered back at Cleopatra lying naked on the bed.

Nobody's ever going to believe this happened, she thought, shaking her head.

Then she peered over at the huge stack of coins and artifacts lying on the floor of the fishing vessel. She reached out and picked up a coin, noticing the queen's image on one side and Marc Antony's on the other, with the date inscribed along the outer edge.

I suppose she won't miss just one, Riley said, slipping the medallion into her pocket before tapping the glass screen. Within a matter of seconds, the time machine started shaking and the familiar swirling funnel cloud emerged atop the surface, causing her hair to dance about her head. As she raised her hand toward the edge of the cloud and began to feel her body pulled inside, she took one last look at the beautiful queen and blew her a kiss.

"Goodbye, my queen," she said. "I wish you well. May history remember you as you were, and may your final resting place remain shrouded in mystery."

As she tumbled through the portal, wondering where she'd end up next, she smiled, knowing that she hadn't changed the course of history as much as she feared. Marc Antony and Cleopatra had still been defeated by the emperor who would become Augustus, the two lovers' grave sites would never be found, and no one would really know how Cleopatra eventually died.

A few seconds later, Riley felt her body thump down into the saddle of some kind of speeding motorcycle, while she careened from side to side, tracking another speeding vehicle through a futuristic cityscape.

"Where the hell am I *now*?" she muttered to herself, suddenly realizing she was dressed in a head-to-toe, tight-fitting leather bodysuit, wearing a futuristic helmet with a heads-up display.

Then she glanced down, realizing her motorcycle didn't have any wheels and that she was riding on a cushion of air, jetting through space on some kind of rocket-propelled jet-ski.

"Well at least I'm properly *dressed* for the occasion this time," she smiled, angling her body while she darted after the levitating motorcycle directly in front of her.

***

Ready *for more steamy chills and thrills? Read the next exciting volume in Riley's Time Travel Adventures, Bounty Hunter. Buy direct and save at victoriarusherotica. Or download from your favorite online bookstore here: retailer links.*

On the lawless planet of Zemius, there's a black market for everything...

ALSO BY VICTORIA RUSH

Adult Fairytales:

The Enchanted Forest: An Erotic Fairytale

The Land of Giants: An Erotic Fairytale

The Dragon's Lair: An Erotic Fairytale

Witch's Brew: An Erotic Fairytale

The Mage's Spell: An Erotic Fairytale

The Mermaid Lagoon: An Erotic Fairytale

The Coven: An Erotic Fairytale

Rapunzel: An Erotic Fairytale

The Seven Dwarfs: An Erotic Fairytale

The Land of Mutants: An Erotic Fairytale

The Erotic Temple: A Sexy Fairytale (Coming Soon)

Erotica Themed Bundles:

Voyeur: Lesbian Erotica Bundle

Public Affairs: A Lesbian Anthology

Futa Fantasies: The Ladyboy Collection

Threesomes: The Lesbian Collection

Threesomes - Volume 2: The Lesbian Collection

First Time: A Lesbian Anthology

Hedonism: An Erotic Anthology

Switch Hitters: Bisexual Erotica

Taboo Erotica: The Lesbian Series

BDSM: The Lesbian Collection

Party Games: The Erotic Collection

Party Games 2: The Erotic Collection

All Girl 1: Lesbian Erotica Bundle

All Girl 2: Lesbian Erotica Bundle

All Girl 3: Lesbian Erotica Bundle

All Girl 4: Lesbian Erotica Bundle

Erotic Fairytale Bundles:

Clover's Fantasy Adventures: Books 1 - 5

Clover's Fantasy Adventures: Books 6 - 10

Erotic Fantasy:

Pirate's Bounty: A Time Travel Adventure

Wild West: A Time Travel Adventure

Private Riley: A Time Travel Adventure

Cleopatra's Secret: A Time Travel Adventure

Bounty Hunter 2125: A Time Travel Adventure

Ninja Assassin: A Time Travel Adventure

The 300: A Time Travel Adventure

Arabian Nights: An Erotic Fairytale (coming soon...)

Steamy Time Travel Bundles:

Riley's Time Travel Adventures: Books 1 - 5

Lesbian Erotica:

The Dinner Party: Lesbian Voyeur Erotica

The Darkroom: Bisexual Voyeur Erotica

Naked Yoga: Lesbian Transgender Erotica

Nude Cruise: Bisexual Voyeur Erotica

Rush Hour: Taboo Public Sex

The Girl Next Door: First Time Lesbian Erotic Romance

Girls' Camp: Lesbian Group Sex

Wet Dream: Ladyboy Fantasy Erotica

The Convent: Taboo Sex with a Nun

Sex Robot: A Dream Sex Machine

The Personal Trainer: Getting Pumped at the Gym

The Dominatrix: BDSM Lesbian Domination

Webcam Chat: Lesbian Online Sex

Paint Me: A Kinky Bodypainting Workshop

The Toy Party: Girls Sharing Sex Toys

The Costume Party: Strapping One On

Swedish Sauna: Lesbian Group Sex

The Therapist: Taboo Lesbian Erotica

Elevator Shaft: Bisexual Threesomes Erotica

Ladyboy: Lesbian Transgender Erotica

Peep Show: Lesbian Voyeur Erotica

The Dare: Public Sex Erotica

Maid Service: Lesbian Threesomes Erotica

The Hitchhiker: First Time Lesbian Erotica

The Housesitter: Spycam Lesbian Erotica

The Spa: Lesbian Group Orgy

Parlor Games: Blindfold Sex Party

The Exchange Student: First Time Lesbian Erotica

The Hostel: Bisexual Group Erotica

The Harem: Lesbian Erotic Romance

The Orient Express: Lesbian Voyeur Erotica

The First Lady: A Forbidden Lesbian Erotic Romance

The Slave: Lesbian BDSM Erotica

The Masseuse: Lesbian Sensuous Erotica

Too Close for Comfort: Lesbian Forbidden Erotica

Naked Twister: A Wild Party Game

Lexi: The Sex App (Lesbian Fantasy Erotica)

Call Girl: Lesbian Bisexual Threesomes Erotica

Circle Jill: Lesbian Masturbation Workshop

The Viewing Room: Masturbation Voyeur Erotica

Spin the Bottle: A Kinky Party Game

The Hair Salon: Lesbian Voyeur Erotica

Tribadism 1: Girls Only Sex Workshop

Tribadism 2: The Art of Scissoring

Tribadism 3: Threeway Hookups

The Kiss: A Game of Oral Sex

Pledge Week: Sorority Sisters

Carny Games 1: A Wild Sex Party

Carny Games 2: A Kinky Sex Party

Carny Games 3: An Erotic Sex Party

Dreamscape: An Artificial Reality Game

Glory Hole: Guess Who's On the Other Side

Joy Ride: A Late Night Erotic Bus Trip

The Blind Girl: An Erotic Romance(Coming Soon)

Lesbian Erotica Bundles:

Jade's Erotic Adventures: Books 1 - 5

Jade's Erotic Adventures: Books 6 - 10

Jade's Erotic Adventures: Books 11 - 15

Jade's Erotic Adventures: Books 16 - 20

Jade's Erotic Adventures: Books 21 - 25

Jade's Erotic Adventures: Books 26 - 30

Standalone Stories:

The Polynesian Girl: A Lesbian EroticRomance